Timegazer

Moses Solomon

Timegazer
© 2013 by Alexander F. Lee

cover illustration by Dana Henderson
© 2013 by Dana Henderson
All Rights Reserved

ISBN 978-0-9894902-2-1
eISBN 978-0-9894902-4-5

Printed in the United States of America

For My Father, and In Memory of My Mother,
For a Lifetime of Love

My sincere thanks go to my editor, Mason McCann Smith, for all his insightful feedback, and Dana Henderson, for his inspiring artwork.

Additional thanks go to Suzy Vitello, Lesann Berry, The Rev. Sara Fischer, and Maureen Kay; Steve Malick; Michael Stack; C.S. Cole, Andrea Letourneau, Mary Rosenblum, and Ron Root; Margo Ander, Allan Anderson, Kyle Fahrbach, Sandra Grace, Andy Jones, Satnam Kaur Khalsa, Karin Ott Kristensen, Gregg Macklin, and Amie Waller; and Blake Swensen and Terry Light for all the helpful comments on the journey to publication.

Prologue

Morgan reached over the steering controls, pulled a small lever, and activated the little Buggy craft's hyperdrive. Beyond the front window, the fabric of space sheared open like a gaping maw, revealing a gray void with pinpoint lights that whisked across the side windows. On the rearview monitor, mounted on top of the dashboard, the streaking lights of the void disappeared into a tiny patch of stars in the distance. He reached down to the center console, switched on the autopilot, and released the yoke.

Glancing sideways at Rayna, Morgan said, "Alone at last."

Rayna unfastened her straps and wrapped her arms around Morgan's neck. He closed his eyes when he felt the warmth of her soft skin. She ran her fingers through his hair, which he kept barely short enough to avoid violating the military dress code. Her cheek snuggled against his, and her dark, wavy, shoulder-length hair settled over his shoulders. She hummed a soft melody as she brushed a tuft of his dark hair from his forehead.

He opened his eyes and gazed at her. "Six months was too long."

Six months apart while Rayna's cruiser, *Pouton*, escorted Alscrasian merchants through pirate-infested routes along the perimeter of the Great Nebula. Six months of passing messages through the intermittent relays of the comm-exchanges while his cruiser, *Ocelot*, patrolled the Alscrasian border.

That Morgan served under Rayna's father made things "interesting."

Captain Choff had never warmed to Morgan in the two years since he and Rayna had graduated from the academy. When they began their assignments, Rayna had asked Morgan to be understanding of her father. At first, he tried, accepting any and every assignment given. But after the captain ordered Morgan down to the hot, cramped engine room to inventory spare parts—tedium appropriate for an enlisted recruit, but not for an officer—and then reprimanded him for reporting back without changing into a clean uniform, all effort at understanding jettisoned out the disposal tube.

"Captain Chump" reminded Morgan of a mercurial foreman he had once apprenticed under who had favored some while coming down hard on others. Though he worked hard and had risen to become second officer in a short time, Morgan felt certain the tension existed because the captain didn't care for his only child's relationship with a guy from the working-class streets of Alscras.

Now, with both of their ships tied up at the same space fortress for maintenance work, Morgan and Rayna finally had an opportunity to go on leave together. The trip to Toutle, a nearby resort world of the far-flung Onglan League, would take a full day. Except for a close passage to Volon, a sparsely populated planet the wormhole curved around, the trip should be uneventful.

Rayna whispered in his ear, "Where did we leave off six months ago?"

She gave his ear a gentle nibble, and Morgan's desire swept over him. He flashed a hungry smile, undid his straps, tossed them aside—and with them, his shirt—and pressed her close. Her top fluttered to the floor, landing on top of his. Their lips met and they pulled themselves out of the pilot's seat and down to the floor.

A violent jolt rocked the spacecraft, interrupting Morgan and Rayna's climactic moment.

"*Dox!*" Morgan cursed as an alarm blared. Nothing could be more annoying than to be stopped by a blown engine relay. But alone out here in space, anything more than that would be a real problem.

Another alarm sounded as a mass of multicolored particles streaked past the front window. A tremor shook the little ship, forcing Rayna to brace herself against the back of her seat. Outside the window, the layered folds of hyperspace collapsed around them, and a starfield settled into place.

Morgan's mind raced. What kind of particle beam could break out of normal space? Checking the monitor, he saw the blue-green world of Volon come into view just as another beam—one that covered the entire width of the front window—fired from the planet. "Hang on, Rayna!" The strike sent rough shivers through the craft.

"Who's shooting at us?" Rayna checked the telemetry data from the shot.

This was one mystery Morgan wanted no part of. The Buggy broadcast no military signals, and to his knowledge, Volon was not advanced enough to build a weapon like this. He switched off the autopilot, took hold of the steering yoke, and fired the boosters to pull the craft away from Volon. "Get the life-suits."

Rayna reached up and released the overhead compartment, allowing two bright orange emergency jumpsuits to roll out. She tossed Morgan's bundle onto the helmet hook next to him, and she quickly donned her suit, fastening the quick-action seals and hanging the helmet on the hook next to her side of the console.

"Can this Buggy take all this?" Rayna strapped herself into her seat and took the controls.

"Don't know." Morgan quickly zipped into his jumpsuit and strapped himself back into his seat. "*Tatiki!*" he cursed, struggling with the steering. "The handling stinks."

"I *told* you to take the Comet," Rayna scolded, "instead of this piece of—"

A wide, twisting band of light, streaming all the colors of the rainbow, lanced out from Volon and smothered the front and side windows, completely enveloping the Buggy. A hot-pink bolt of energy leaped out from a vent, arced across the instrument panel, and struck the bank of data monitors, shorting out two of the gauges in a shower of sparks. Morgan's hands jerked loose from the yoke as the bolt flashed through the steering column.

He pivoted his head at the sound of Rayna's scream. Struck by the bolt in a blinding flash of light, she lurched into convulsions.

"Rayna!"

Rayna slumped in her seat, unconscious.

A red alarm annunciator flashed on the dashboard. In the center of the instrument panel, the gyro-stabilizer erupted in a cloud of black smoke. A second later, the main engine blew out with a booming concussion that blasted the back wall, propelling a shower of smoking shrapnel through the cockpit.

"*Shat'oq!*" Morgan cursed as he watched the planet spiral toward them.

They fell toward the equator like a meteor. With one hand clamped like a vise on the steering gear, Morgan reached over with his other hand to yank Rayna's crash restraints over her, snapping the full-body harnesses over her regular seat straps. He hit the emergency signal to broadcast an automated distress code in all Imperial dialects, then secured his own emergency restraints.

"Stay with me, Rayna." Coaxing the last vestiges of power from the crippled engine, Morgan tried to steady the ship's descent with short thruster bursts and a steely hand on the yoke. "Come on!" he urged the Buggy.

Miraculously, the craft righted itself just before entering the upper atmosphere. Morgan fought to keep the craft stable as it glided down. Sweat broke out under his jumpsuit. On the front window, the fiery friction of the craft streaking through the atmosphere obscured his view of the descent. The automatic temperature alarm sounded an alert each time the cabin temp increased an additional five degrees. Soon, the air started to feel suffocating.

Morgan glanced over at Rayna. She lay limp under her restraints, her eyes still closed, her breathing remaining slow though steady. With some systems on the blink and others totally dark, he could barely maintain his precarious hold over the craft's descent.

The Buggy emerged through the clouds, and when the heat broke, the temp alerts ceased. Bright sunlight gave Morgan a clear view of the landscape. A snow-peaked mountain range passed by below them. Beyond lay a vast forest. Keeping his eyes glued to the flight path ahead, Morgan reached overhead and switched on the automatic landing sequence. No data appeared on the ground-tracking monitor; not even a beep sounded. He tried the switch again. Again, no response. He looked up and saw black scorch-marks along the edge of the panel.

"*Dox!*"

The forest rushed toward them, and he drew in a deep breath to steel his nerves against the inevitable crash landing. Morgan gave Rayna one more glance. Her helmet was hanging out of his reach. He pulled his own helmet off its hook and slapped it over her head, the magnetic seals fastening.

Now close enough to see individual trees whisk by, he tried to steady his breathing. His heartbeat raced as he guided them down the last few feet.

The craft mowed down a line of treetops, the rough bumps jarring the ride down. Without warning, the trees gave way, revealing a formation of jagged boulders marking a break in the forest. Everything jumped with a loud concussion as the base of the craft hit the tallest boulder. The craft toppled at an awkward angle. The force of the impact jerked and twisted Morgan against his emergency straps. The steering yoke yanked out of his grasp, nearly ripping his hands from his wrists. The Buggy hit the ground and bounced several times, part of the dashboard erupting into another cloud of foul black smoke. The overhead landing control panel burst out in an explosive flash of energy and tumbled down on Morgan.

Amidst the chaos, he reached out for her. "Rayna—"

As the tumbling panel struck his head, an old proverb flashed in his mind: *At the end of life, the souls that follow Almighty Euranus will find Eurania.* Then he blacked out.

1. The Shaman

"Rayna?"

Morgan's voice was barely audible. His head throbbed with pain. A stinging sensation radiated from his shoulders down his arms, and a dull ache racked his chest from the tug of the restraints. A blur of red and yellow lights blinked on the dashboard, indicating a complete failure. Unsure of how long he had been unconscious, Morgan took a long, slow breath and waited for his vision to clear.

Two sections of the dashboard still smoldered. As the pain began to subside, he turned on the vent to blow some of the thick smoke out of the craft. The astro-nav computer read: Memory reset. He rubbed his head with his hand and found it smeared with blood. The distress signal that he had activated as they went down had stopped, the comm unit dead. This was not how their leave was supposed to be.

"Rayna?" He turned his head.

Her seat was empty, the unfastened straps dangling down the sides. Her helmet lay on the floor.

He gasped, his heart racing. What had happened while he was out? He ripped his buckles open, threw his straps aside, staggered to his feet, and scanned the cockpit wreckage. The overhead panel lay on the floor behind his seat, dented and scarred with black scorches from the blowout, with a tiny smear of blood from Morgan's head.

"Rayna!"

Morgan looked at the tousled pile of clothes on the floor, his hands trembling, his heart pounding like a cannon, a nauseous panic rising up.

Then he saw it—the airlock was ajar, opened wide enough for a person to fit through. The doorframe itself was cracked, apparently broken during the crash. There!

He opened the locker, grabbed the belt with his gun and the charcoal-gray vest that held a pair of short silver skiloblades, and fastened them on. Then he put on his lightweight jacket over the vest and the weapons. The jacket's dark umber color would conceal his bright orange top and help him blend into the surrounding forest, in case he encountered hostile Volonians or animals. Now ready, he climbed through the broken airlock and stepped out.

Morgan plunged into the forest, his eyes

scanning the thick layers of dark green foliage, broken branches, and splintered tree trunks, looking for a sign of Rayna. He knew nothing about the people of Volon or why modern development had seemed to skip over this planet. Volon wasn't unique. There were plenty of lush worlds throughout the Euranian star cluster. However, those that remained undeveloped lay along the perimeter of the Outer Territories, not situated within an organized region like the Onglan League. Obviously, Volon wasn't as primitive as the reports indicated. He struggled with conflicting thoughts of what to do should he encounter a Volonian.

Movement in a nearby clearing caught Morgan's eye. He sneaked close enough to make out three humans standing together. Two men in skullcaps—a muscular one with red lightning bolts tattooed on both arms and a bulky firearm hanging from his belt, and another in a short brown robe covered by a metallic jacket sporting a spider print—had their backs to Morgan. A woman in an off-white cape with a similar spider image and a hood was speaking to them in low tones, in an unfamiliar language.

Native Volonian tongue, Morgan guessed. Since Volon sat within the borders of the Onglan League, Morgan decided to try the lower-Onglan dialect that he had learned during his academy years. He knew he would speak with a peculiar accent, but it didn't matter. He cleared his throat and approached them.

One of the Volonian men stepped away, giving Morgan a clear view of the Volonian woman as she knelt down to the grass, next to the body of a woman lying on the ground in an orange jumpsuit.

Rayna!

The woman bent down and put her hands over his beloved's face. As Morgan broke into a sprint toward them, a faint golden glow began to emanate from the woman's hands, bathing Rayna's head in a warm field of light. Without warning, a web of blinding sparks filled the halo, covering Rayna's face with static.

Morgan yelled in Onglan, "What are you doing to her?" He instinctively reached under his jacket and whipped out his charge-lock gun, his fingers flipping the switch to arm the weapon's charge-pak loader. "Get away!"

The tattooed Volonian drew his firearm and pointed it at Morgan.

The woman stood and held up her hands. "Thakian, no." The glow in her hands faded away.

For an instant, Morgan thought he saw a red light in her brown eyes. He glanced down at Rayna, her face no longer enveloped in the woman's field of light. Rayna's eyes were closed, and she lay unconscious, as she had been in the Buggy.

The armored man stepped forward, shouldering Thakian aside to speak to Morgan. "The woman is hurt." He spoke in a lightly accented Onglan. "We brought her from the wreckage so that Jairesse can help her."

Morgan hesitated, unsure. Could he believe them? He had heard stories of races outside the empire exhibiting unusual abilities—some that healed, some that killed. He knelt next to Rayna, took her hand, and felt for her pulse. Slow, faint, but what alarmed him was the coolness of her skin. Anything was possible, and he struggled to think objectively.

Kneeling next to Morgan, Jairesse spoke in a soft, even tone. "She will not awaken without my help." She removed her hood and straightened her long, wavy blonde hair. "If I do not help her now, she will soon die."

Morgan's gaze swung from Volonian to Volonian. His fingers itched on the trigger, but he took a deep breath to steady himself. "What's her condition? What can you do for her?"

He heard a long, deep gasp; his eyes returned to Rayna, his free hand still holding hers. Had she stopped breathing? Seconds passed, and then Rayna gasped again. He squeezed her hand, his fingers rubbing hers. Again, she seemed to stop breathing. Then she gasped again.

If Jairesse was telling the truth, and he prevented her from helping, and Rayna died, he could never live with himself. His eyes moistening, he lowered his hands and nodded. "If any harm comes to her…" He paused, aware of the rapid beat of his heart, the throbbing pain of his headache, and the tremble in his hands. "Sorry." His sweaty palms tightened on his gun. "She is…very special to me."

"I understand." Jairesse removed her cape, revealing a golden robe. "What is her name?"

"Rayna." Clearing his throat, Morgan said, "Her name is Rayna Choff."

The armored man stepped forward and held out his hands. "I am Adonair."

Morgan eyed Adonair, then Jairesse, and finally Thakian, still holding his firearm, still suspicious. "Morgan Teggo." So far, the Volonians seemed friendly enough, a touch old-fashioned with their natural-fiber clothing and their small electronic items either attached to their waists or hanging from their necks. It was all consistent with what he thought Volonians might be like. Could he trust them? "Please, help her."

Jairesse knelt at Rayna's side with one hand hovering over Rayna's forehead and the other over Rayna's chest. She closed her eyes for a few seconds, then stood back up and said to Adonair and Thakian, "Please gather seven *quellates*."

The two men immediately ran into the forest.

Jairesse told Morgan, "Place her hands across her chest."

Staying on guard, Morgan put his gun down, took Rayna's hands, and crossed them over her heart. Then he took up his gun again, and they waited in silence, Morgan holding out hope for a sudden revival without any further intervention.

Adonair and Thakian soon returned with plant specimens, which they handed to Jairesse.

She turned to Morgan and held out the seven plant specimens to him. "Place this large purple vine across her collar, this small golden flower over her forehead, this red stem in the grasp of her right hand…"

Morgan hesitated, unsure of what Jairesse had in mind. The flowers appeared plain and ordinary, like decorative pieces. These were the *quellates*?

He re-holstered his gun under his vest and accepted the plant samples. He laid the purple vine across Rayna's collar and placed the golden flower on her forehead. He gently opened the fingers of her right hand and wrapped them around the red stem. As he continued, he kept his eyes on Rayna's face. Her gasps for breath seemed to be less frequent, the ominous stretches of utter stillness longer.

Morgan didn't see how a handful of flowers could help, and he struggled with the foreboding feeling that he might lose Rayna, but he couldn't deny the brief display of power Jairesse had exhibited—whatever that had been. He wished he understood what was going on and how, exactly, Jairesse's primitive setup would save Rayna. When he finished placing all seven specimens, he stepped back and waited with bated breath.

Jairesse knelt, held her hands close to either side of Rayna's head, and took several deep breaths. A faint glow emerged in the palms of her hands.

Jairesse tilted her head back and raised her arms skyward, her sleeves falling aside to reveal glowing silver bracelets with etchings of unfamiliar symbols. She began uttering a soft melodic chant that flowed as smoothly as gentle waves of water.

"Ooooo, kha'tha, duolu, Oscanos, kha'tha, duolu, Gheriah, pan'dithy."

Morgan had no clue what Jairesse was doing. The chant felt almost musical. Rayna loved to sing. Was this Jairesse's way of reaching Rayna's brain activity? Would the glowing hands warm Rayna? He squeezed his fists to steady himself and calm his nerves.

"Ooooo, kha'tha, duolu, kaandathi, maandathi, pan'dithy."

Jairesse brought her arms down, her glowing hands together, lowered her head so that her face disappeared behind a cascade of her golden hair, and dropped her voice to a whisper that felt primitive, almost pre-human.

"Hicith, cislema, jaka-jaka..."

The chant no longer felt soothing to Morgan. Instead, it now sounded like rodent murmurings, animalistic.

Rayna's face remained unchanged, unmoving, as if resting in peace.

Jairesse placed one hand on the top of Rayna's head, the other on her waist, and her singing changed to a soft atonal wordless melody.

Morgan crossed his arms to steady their tremble.

His heart pounded, and he felt a drop of perspiration slither down his side. He recognized two words from Jairesse's chant. *Oscanos* and *Gheriah* were the names of two deities of the mythological pantheon that many Euranians—both those who resided within the Central Empire and those outside —still worshipped. As far back as he could remember, he had never believed the ancient stories. But even aboard *Ocelot*, many did.

Morgan shook his head at the sight of Jairesse kneeling beside Rayna, the glow from her hands spreading over Rayna's body to form a halo. This was not the sort of modern medical treatment Rayna needed. If he could only get her back to the space fortress, she would be in better hands. This was religion, nothing more, and Rayna's life lay in the hands of a shaman.

Hours passed. Adonair and Thakian silently sat with their backs against nearby trees. Jairesse and Rayna remained unchanged, the chanting continuing in a low whisper. The sun, having passed overhead, began to set, the shadows of the forest lengthening, the air beginning to cool.

Morgan's muscles had stiffened from the tension, and his head felt bruised from the bump. He was exhausted. Feelings of hope and helplessness jumbled his thoughts. He could only keep watch over Rayna. How long could he wait for Jairesse and her mystic ritual? But he had no choice. They were stranded; he had to take the chance that Jairesse might be right.

He was tired. He couldn't decide what was best for Rayna. He had to stay strong, for himself and for her.

At twilight, Jairesse opened her eyes, and the glow faded away. She took three deep breaths and rose to her feet. Rayna still lay next to Morgan, unchanged. With a sweep of her hand, Jairesse brushed the plant specimens to the grass.

Morgan jumped to his feet, startled by the sudden move. "Is she…all right?"

"Her injuries were severe," Jairesse said, donning her cape. "She is still healing within, but she should recover with time, adequate rest, and no further stress." She gently placed her hand—now without any trace of the glowing light—on Morgan's arm. "You can relax. Your beloved will live."

Morgan desperately wanted to believe Jairesse, but he did not see anything that looked different about Rayna.

"When will she awaken?"

"She may be able to hear you." Jairesse stepped away. "Perhaps you can awaken her."

"Rayna?" He could only hope. He knelt at her side, took her hand, and spoke to her in Alscrasian. "Rayna? It's Morgan. I'm right here. Hey, you're going to be fine." He brought her hand to his face. It felt reasonably warm. He felt her pulse. Slow and steady. "Can you hear me in your dreams?" He let out a nervous chuckle. "*Dox*, your father's going to have my head, for sure. What should we tell him?"

He watched her chest rise and fall. Her breathing now seemed steady and normal. If he didn't know the truth of the situation, he would have guessed that she was simply in deep sleep, without any ill effects. But she still wasn't responding. He could still lose her, and the thought terrified him. "Come back to me, please." His voice cracked.

He held her hands in his, closed his eyes, and lowered his head. *If there was any truth to the Euranian Ancestors, now would be a good time for them to show themselves and save her.*

"Morgan...?"

His eyes flew open—and hers were open, too. "Rayna!" He squeezed her hands, excited, relieved, grateful, his heart pounding. *It wasn't too much to ask for.* Morgan bent down and gave her a gentle kiss.

"Wait." Rayna took in the mass of trees and boulders surrounding them. "Where are we?" She looked confused, then a look of recognition appeared. "The particle beam..."

"How do you feel?" *First things first.*

She took in a deep breath. "Tired." Still on the ground, she wiggled her arms and torso. "Stiff, sore, but not painful." She quickly put her hand on his chest. "Is this Volon?"

Morgan helped Rayna up, then motioned toward Jairesse. Switching to Onglan, he introduced, "Your healer, Jairesse." He paused, remembering all the doubts he had harbored throughout her ritual. He didn't understand what happened, but whatever Jairesse did, it worked. "I don't know how I can thank you."

Jairesse crossed her arms. "You may consider relaxing your guard. You are among friends."

Morgan lowered his eyes and nodded.

"Thank you," Rayna said to Jairesse. She bowed and came back up, lightheaded.

"Whoa!" Morgan quickly caught Rayna in his arms.

"Sorry," Rayna said with an embarrassed smile as she steadied herself.

"Please take care," Jairesse cautioned. "You are still recovering."

As a full moon rose over the nearby mountain range, Morgan introduced Adonair and Thakian to Rayna, who immediately began peppering the Volonians with questions about what had happened to her.

Jairesse stepped forward, her hand up, interrupting Rayna's questions. "Your *suromila* was blocked," she said.

Morgan didn't recognize the word. Was it more of Jairesse's mysticism? He glanced at Rayna, who looked lost.

"My what?" she asked.

"The center of your being," Jairesse explained as she sat down on the ground. Adonair and Thakian followed suit, sitting on either side of her. "It is what makes human beings different from all other animal life. Another day, and your life force would have deteriorated to the point of death." She paused and spread her arms out. "We who are humans are connected to the *Pankoulda*."

Hearing yet more unfamiliar Volonian babble, Morgan waved Rayna over.

"What is it?" Rayna asked him.

"You're not going to get anything useful from her," Morgan said, nodding his head toward Jairesse. "Just a lot of obscure Volonian religion."

Rayna stared at Jairesse. "I want to hear it." She walked back, sat down with the others, and waited for Jairesse to continue.

After thinking it over, Morgan also sat to listen.

"Deep in the center of our being," Jairesse began, "the *Pankoulda* reach across space and time to regenerate our life force with their thoughts. When you are alone and very quiet, you can sense their presence. Not just our animate life energy but our intelligence springs from the *Pankoulda*. Our thoughts, our feelings, all of our emotional bonds with one another."

Morgan looked away. It was all mystical talk, matters he never gave much credence to. As a platoon officer, Rayna was used to encountering native life and their unfamiliar ways, so he wasn't surprised that she wanted to listen. But Rayna was always too headstrong, and he didn't see how Jairesse's religious exposition connected to what had happened to Rayna.

"With your *suromila* blocked, you were no longer connected to the *Pankoulda*, the source of higher life." Jairesse paused. "Do you understand? Your mind and soul cannot live without the sustaining presence of the *Pankoulda*. Even though your bodily functions could be mechanically maintained, you—Rayna Choff—would have ceased to exist."

Rayna ran her hand over the grass, her gaze following the movement of the blades. "So, I was fortunate to have been found by someone like you who understood all this."

Jairesse nodded. "You are restored now. You only need to regain your strength."

Morgan eyed Jairesse, Rayna having voiced exactly what he was thinking. He would be forever grateful that she had saved Rayna, but Jairesse's choice of words in describing the possibility of Rayna's death was too foreign for him to accept. If Rayna hadn't been physically injured, would she have died of an empty mind? This Volonian woman was still a mystery—perhaps too mysterious for comfort. "Forgive my ignorance, Jairesse, but... who are you?"

Jairesse only smiled at Morgan.

Adonair said, "She is the priestess of our temple. What she explained to you is privileged knowledge that's been passed down from the ancient days." He crossed his arms. "Who are you, and where are you from?"

Morgan said, "Obviously, not from Volon." Adonair's question was fair enough, a crash landing in their forest probably not a common occurrence. "We were shot down by a powerful particle beam. You must have seen it?"

"Are you referring to the *Hruvrah*?" Thakian asked. "It sent shock waves throughout the valley."

"*Hruvrah*?" Morgan asked, raising an eyebrow.

Thakian made an arc-shaped motion with his arm. "The rainbow of the gods."

"Rainbow…" Morgan remembered the particle beam exhibiting rainbowlike colors. "The beam that hit us was a straight shot from the ground into space." He caught Adonair glancing toward a distinctive twin peak in the mountains. Did the Volonians know something? "What's the *Hruvrah*?"

After a brief but awkward pause among the Volonians, Jairesse spoke. "It is a prophecy. Its appearance marks the beginning of a period of turmoil and conflict unseen since the ancient days." Her face turned ominous as she spoke. "As the priestess of our temple, it is my duty to seek out the Timegazer and learn what is to come upon us."

Morgan shook his head and looked at the

ground. He didn't believe in any religious prophecies, local or interstellar. But the so-called *Hruvrah* was the particle beam that had nearly killed him and Rayna. He had to find out who was behind it and why it had fired at a passing Buggy that posed no threat. An advanced weapon among these simple people just didn't make sense.

"A subject strictly for the temple," Adonair quickly interjected. "You need not be concerned about it."

Morgan paused. Adonair's curt response was disturbing, especially after all of Jairesse's lifesaving help and friendliness. Was Adonair harboring a secret? Morgan glanced at Rayna to see if she'd picked up on anything they'd said. Switching to Alscrasian, he said, "I need to think a little bit. Are you feeling well enough to stand?"

Rayna nodded with a reassuring smile.

Switching back to Onglan, Morgan said to her, "We should go work on the comm unit." He turned to the Volonians. "We need to call for a rescue, the sooner the better."

After rising to his feet, he helped Rayna up and they walked slowly and deliberately back to the wreckage of the Buggy. Taking deep breaths and swinging his arms, Morgan pondered the Volonians with each step. Especially Adonair.

After stepping back inside the ruined craft, Morgan went straight to the pilot's seat and opened up the receiver, while Rayna retrieved her weapons from the locker. Within minutes, Morgan had panels open, circuits and feeders removed and carefully laid in a row on the floor among the scattering of debris, and the main array component extended from its bay as far as the bent tracks would allow it. He inspected the unit and discovered that a relay set, while intact, had one of its connections jarred loose during the landing. After reconnecting the relay, the receiver began beeping and the monitor displayed a message header on its screen. Relieved that the fix was so simple, Morgan silenced the beeper and opened the full message.

"BG-832, *this is Space Fortress C, acknowledging reception of your distress signal.*

"We are analyzing the craft telemetry attached to your signal. Preliminary indications are that you sustained a time distortion from a particle shower which interfered with the operation of the craft's systems.

"Please send us your current status. Space Fortress out."

Morgan closed the message and sat back in his seat to consider their situation. He looked out the window, past the lush forest, and studied the mountain peaks in the moonlight. The valley lay quiet, with only an occasional animal call in the distance. A flock of small birds with glowing amber eyes flew past a nearby mountain peak. A large flying reptile, also with glowing eyes, glided over the treetops.

He still puzzled over why no one had ever developed this world. Given its location within the territory of the Onglan League and an abundance of natural resources, it would have made sense for the Onglans to establish a presence here, if no one from the Central Empire did. And yet the mysterious particle beam attested to the fact that someone with advanced knowledge was here.

Rayna sat down in her seat and put two cups of water on the dashboard. She pointed at his forehead. "You should bandage that up."

Morgan nodded but kept working on the comm unit. He had enough of a hunch about the Volonians and the particle beam to consider following them. But given Rayna's weakened condition, he felt uncertain about placing her in a potentially dangerous situation.

Rayna took a sip. "You didn't believe a word of what Jairesse said, did you?"

Morgan emptied his cup in one mouthful. "Where is your *suromila*? In your heart?" He held both hands over his chest. "Your brain?" He made a bowl with his hands and placed it over his head. "Your liver?" He thumped his right side. "You know the liver is the energy generator of your body."

She laughed. "I assume *Pankoulda* is just a local name for the Euranian Ancestors."

A thought occurred to him. "You know, we've only Jairesse's word to go on. There's no real data to support her interpretation. When we get back to the space fortress, Dr. Creatoun will check you over. Then we'll know what really happened, and that will be that."

She smiled and nodded. "Okay."

Morgan closed up the panel. "Well, the good news is that the comm's working now. The bad news is that nothing else is." He paused. "I have a hunch I want to follow. The rainbow—"

Rayna held up her hand. "I know what you're thinking—that we need to track down the particle beam. But wouldn't it be better to send for a squad from the space fortress?"

Morgan shook his head. "We don't have enough hard information to request a mission." He looked Rayna over.

"I'm fine, if that's what you're wondering," Rayna said, sounding a bit insistent. "The dizziness is gone. I have no broken bones, and I don't see any of my blood anywhere—unlike someone else we know. If I weren't up to the task, I'd let you know."

Morgan wasn't totally convinced, but Rayna seemed to be regaining her strength. Would she really be up for what amounted to a self-directed investigation? "Well, if we could join these Volonians while they're here with us, they might lead us right to the source of the particle beam." After pausing for one final minute of consideration, he decided to take Rayna at her word. He reached for the transmitter set, adding, "If my hunch is right, that is."

"Just don't report what happened to me," Rayna said. "I don't want my father to get all agitated while we're still here."

"Uh-huh." Brushing aside her concern, Morgan switched on the transmitter. "Space Fortress C, this is *BG-832*, on the surface of Volon, Lieutenant Teggo speaking. Our craft is not flyable, after crash-landing. We await a rescue craft." He glanced over at Rayna, who was mouthing a "no-no-no" gesture at him. "Ensign Choff was briefly knocked unconscious during the crash but is recovered now." This was for her own good, Morgan decided. "She will require a full examination upon our return."

Rayna threw her hands up in disapproval.

"In the meantime, we have met three Volonians who gave us assistance." He glanced at Rayna. She looked steamed. For Morgan, there was no need to report his hunch about following the Volonians just yet. "Teggo out."

He switched off the transmitter and faced Rayna's glare. He'd seen that look before. "Just planning ahead, that's all."

"I hope Dad slaps you down!"

"Rayna…" His brain scrambled to salvage the conversation. The last thing he wanted was another confrontation with Captain Choff and another sentence to the supply room. "I was just thinking of your health. Because I care."

She seemed taken aback. "If you cared, you'd

consider my feelings on matters like these."

Morgan stopped—it was true. He tended to forget that, in many ways, she was his equal. In some things, she was his superior. After all, she was a platoon officer, trained to establish landings in unfamiliar settings, learn about the locals, and deal with hostile encounters.

"You know you're not cleared for duty, don't you?" He softened his voice. "There's no medical officer here."

Rayna frowned. "I told you I'm fine."

Morgan sighed. "You may be a squad leader—"

"*Platoon* leader," Rayna corrected him. "I command three squads."

"—but I still outrank you."

"Not by much."

Morgan didn't want to give in, even though she was just as headstrong as he was. "You're determined, aren't you?" He thought it over. "All right, I'm listening."

"Morgan, I have to come along with you." Her facial muscles were clenched, stern.

Morgan's shoulders slumped.

"I can't just sit here, all alone. I'll go crazy." Now, her voice softened. "I need something like this job to take my mind off of all this."

Morgan sighed; he knew her next line by heart.

She took his hands. "You always make me feel better." She looked into his eyes. "Maybe that's why I love you."

It was no use. Again. "And I love you, too." He gave in, smiling at her. "If Jairesse says you're okay, then I'll be okay with you going."

She jumped out of her seat, threw her arms around him, and gave him a passionate kiss. They pulled themselves out of his seat and down to the floor, picking up where they had been interrupted by the crash.

Morgan and Rayna emerged from their craft, both armed and jacketed. With handheld lights to guide their way through the darkness, they rejoined the three Volonians.

Morgan immediately addressed Jairesse. "It will be about a Volonian day before a rescue craft arrives."

Jairesse turned to face Rayna. "I should examine you before we depart." She peered into Rayna's eyes, placed her hands over Rayna's temples, and waited until a soft golden glow from her hands enveloped Rayna's head.

Morgan held his breath, tense from the sight of Jairesse's red eyes.

"You are whole, but weak," Jairesse pronounced. "Take care to avoid danger, so that nothing disrupts your *suromila*."

"I understand," Rayna said, her voice sounding slightly muffled from within the halo.

Jairesse bowed her head and withdrew her hands. The golden glow faded away, and her eyes returned to normal.

Morgan took Rayna's hand. "Are you sure you feel all right?"

"For the two-hundredth time, I'm fine." There was a hint of annoyance in her voice.

"We should go," Adonair urged Jairesse. "The rest of our party awaits our return with the holy commandments of the Timegazer."

"Yes." Thakian led everyone a short distance through the trees to a smaller clearing, where a big-wheeled, box-shaped transport rover sat.

"Volon is modernized?" Morgan asked, surprised.

"Enough to be practical," Adonair said, opening a panel next to the door. "We receive the interstellar widecasts from the empire. But we're not like you, with advanced spaceships. We live simpler here."

"Wait." Motioning with his hand toward his gun, Morgan said, "We should accompany you into the mountains."

"There's no need." Thakian's face was cold, the muscles of his jaw tensed.

Jairesse smiled, her hand raised to calm Thakian. "Thakian is a Master of the *Illito*, our people's warriors. He will protect me during the journey. And Adonair is also accompanying me." She spread her arms out. "Thank you for your offer. Morgan and Rayna, may the *Pankoulda* bestow their blessings onto you." She bowed to them.

Morgan was about to insist on following when a

sharp howl pierced the cool night air. A flame-red flying reptile, its eyes a bright yellow and its fang-lined jaws gaping, leaped out of a nearby tree and plunged toward them.

"Everyone down!" Morgan yelled. He and Rayna ran to opposing sides of the clearing, their charge-lock guns in hand.

Jairesse screamed as she and Adonair dove for cover under the rover chassis. Thakian pivoted to face the predator, his firearm drawn, but had to dive to the ground as the beast swiped at him with its massive talons.

"Fire!" Morgan ordered.

He and Rayna pummeled the flying reptile from both sides, catching it in a crossfire of high-energy shots until it crashed to the ground in a bloody, smoking heap, its final, dying cries echoing through the forest.

Morgan approached the animal, his gun still pointed at it. "Thakian? Are you okay?"

Thakian only huffed with disgust as he got to his feet, ignoring Morgan, while Rayna helped Jairesse and Adonair out from under the rover.

"It's dead." Morgan gave the smoldering reptile a firm nudge with his foot. The stench of burning flesh drifted through the air. He eyed Thakian, then turned to face Jairesse. "Are you sure you don't want us to accompany you?"

2. *The Fountain of Eternal Passage*

Morgan peered over Thakian's shoulder at the front window of the transport rover. Outside, the forest was thinning, revealing the foothills of an abrupt mountain range. The ride became bumpy as the terrain grew jagged, littered with bare rock. Steep, craggy formations shot two thousand feet skyward, where low-lying charcoal-gray clouds drifted past pointed peaks that occasionally blocked the moonlight.

Thakian gave Morgan a hard stare, cold enough to make Morgan back off. Morgan knew that he and Rayna needed to tread lightly. Jairesse had overruled both Thakian and Adonair on bringing Morgan and Rayna along, and while both Volonian men were obedient, they were obviously resentful.

"How do you do this?" Morgan turned and asked Jairesse, his hands held up, emulating her. "Are there others who have the same power as you?"

Jairesse shook her head. "Only one other, and she is very young. Very undisciplined and childlike, but she is learning well for her age. Someday, she will succeed me. It is her calling."

Soon, the rover drove up the rocky incline and onto a mountain pass. One side rose straight up, a sheer wall; the other side fell into a steep chasm. Morgan peered out the window and saw the surging rapids of a dark green river far below. A giant brown sea snake flailed in the foam. They reached the end of the drivable pass, a cul-de-sac flanked by drops on both sides. A vertical wall towered before them. After pointing the rover's headlights at a small cave-like opening recessed ten feet up in the wall, they disembarked from the vehicle.

"I don't like this." Thakian scanned about in all directions with his handlight, grunted at Adonair, and drew his firearm. "Wait here."

Morgan put his hand on Thakian's shoulder. "You're not going alone, are you?"

Thakian shrugged Morgan's hand away. "I am a Master of the *Illito*."

"Let us go with you," Rayna said.

"It is my purpose," Thakian said with a stern face. "It is my honor."

Morgan was stuck. Whatever rank Thakian held, they had outclassed him earlier, and Morgan didn't want to heap more insult on a tradition-bound mindset. "This may be more than a one-person job."

Thakian shook his head.

Morgan looked at Adonair and Jairesse, both stoic, and gave in. "All right, we don't want to be disrespectful."

Thakian grunted, turned away, and climbed the giant rocks with an athletic agility that impressed Morgan. Within seconds, Thakian reached the opening. After peering inside with his handlight, Thakian proceeded into the cave.

Within seconds, a desperate cry sounded from within.

"Thakian!" Jairesse yelled.

Morgan and Rayna drew their guns, bounded up the boulders, charged into the cave, and paused a moment for their eyes to adjust to the utter darkness. They pulled handlights out of their jacket pockets and flipped them on, Rayna's pointed ahead into the darkness, Morgan's swinging from side to side at an assortment of animal-head statues and other ruins lining the walls.

As they rounded the corner, Rayna pointed at a shadowy figure running away into the distance.

"Wait," Morgan said, nearly tripping over a body. He stooped down and shone his light on the face. "*Krok*! It's Thakian!"

He and Rayna sprang into defensive positions over Thakian's body, their lights scanning about them, their guns at the ready.

Adonair and Jairesse ran in and knelt beside Thakian. Jairesse cradled his head. Morgan glanced down and saw Thakian's eyes settle into narrow slits, his head limp in Jairesse's hands.

"Jairesse..." Thakian murmured, barely audible. He suddenly coughed up a mouthful of blood, his body convulsing as he began choking. "The Xaturi..."

"Thakian!" She looked to Adonair, her eyes pleading for help.

Adonair picked up Thakian's light and shone it on Thakian's now-pale face. Thakian calmed, and Jairesse felt for a pulse along his neck, but after a few seconds, she could only shake her head.

"Thakian..." Her voice trembled. "Don't leave us."

A warm, gentle breeze blew into the cave. It grazed over them, light as feathers, before disappearing into the depths. As it passed, Thakian expired.

"No..." Jairesse's face contorted with sadness, and she lowered Thakian's head. She placed her hand on Thakian's forehead and broke down. With tears streaming down her face, she put the *Illito* warrior's firearm into his right hand, took both of his arms, and crossed them over his chest.

Morgan instinctively put his hand on Jairesse's shoulder and helped her steady herself. He glanced at Rayna and was struck at how she stared at Thakian's face, seemingly lost in thought. If he knew it would be this deadly, he wouldn't have let her come on this trip, not so soon after her brush with death.

He took a step over to Rayna, but when she looked at him and said, "We should move them outside, for safety," he felt reassured that her mind was still on her job.

Jairesse regained her composure with a deep breath. She placed her hand on Thakian's chest, lowered her head, and began chanting.

"Memono G'pathi amenno, Oscanos.

"Thakian potho li dactus, Gheriah.

"Abethi demni..."

Morgan and Rayna stood on guard outside the mouth of the cave, in case the attacker rushed out, while Adonair assisted Jairesse with the last rites for Thakian. Morgan looked away from the scene. Jairesse's whispery words, clearly not Onglan in nature, were completely foreign to him. Rayna, meanwhile, looked lost in contemplation.

"The chanting sounds nothing like the funerals I've been to," Morgan observed.

"Different people from different worlds may have different rites," Rayna reflected.

Adonair approached them. "He was the finest and bravest of our *Illito*." He stared up at the twin-peaked mountain. A passing hawk flew by. "We love peace; we have not had a murderer among our people in over five centuries. Whenever we've found someone killed, we've always traced the killing to a visitor from outside our valley."

Morgan found such a uniform peacefulness intriguing, but unlikely for such a long period of time.

"Long ago," Adonair continued, "our leaders formed an elite corps to educate our people in peaceful ways. They learned and mastered the ancient *Illito* martial arts, but they also followed the *Illito* philosophy of understanding. Though they armed themselves, as all protectors must, they rarely had a confrontation that involved violence. Only intrusions of outsiders have broken the peace; only an outsider could explain the cruel massacre that occurred."

Uncomfortable with seeming insensitive, Morgan debated whether now was the time to question Adonair. But a killer still lurked somewhere inside the cave.

"What did Thakian mean when he said, 'The Xaturi'?" Morgan waited and tried to gauge Adonair's expression.

"The Xaturi..." After several slow breaths, Adonair's voice regained its strength. "This is our matter. You must understand, this is of no concern to you."

Morgan was growing tired of Adonair's evasion. They now had an unforeseen obstacle to finding the source of the particle beam, and Adonair was not helping. On the verge of losing his patience, Morgan struggled to keep his voice steady. "I do understand that this is your concern, not ours. But

Thakian is dead. Jairesse is no warrior. Your priestess could be the next victim. I ask again: What is the Xaturi?"

Adonair's face contorted. He turned away and looked over the chasm, toward a distant mountain range. "It is a killer, a murderer, an evil creature that is supposed to inhabit these mountains but has not been seen in over a millennium."

"Myths and legends don't help," Morgan said. "Why didn't you bring a larger contingent for such a dangerous journey?"

Adonair shook his head. "Coming before the Timegazer is only for our priestess. It is a holy site. Thakian was the best of our warriors, and I am accompanying Jairesse because, as the administrator of the temple, I am already privileged to some of the sacred knowledge. But I will not set foot inside the sanctuary when we reach it." He eyed Morgan and Rayna, then opened a flap on his jacket and brought out several small pieces of paper. "I've been told my sketch is not very similar to the real article, but it was the best I could do, based on the description our ruler's great-uncle gave me." He unfolded one page to reveal a rough drawing of a black reptile with oversized scaly wings and a serpentine tail, accompanied by a line of unfamiliar symbols. Handing the drawing to Morgan and Rayna, he said, "The Xaturi."

After Jairesse concluded the Volonian last rites

for Thakian, Morgan and Rayna helped Adonair carry Thakian's body into the rover. They then reentered the cave, Morgan and Rayna leading the way, Adonair and Jairesse following.

They paused before the statues of humans, semi-humans, and beasts lined up against the wall. Several were human in armor and helmets, with trident weapons in their hands and guns hanging from their belts. Others were tentacled creatures with human heads, large wings, and serpentine tails. Still others looked like amoebas covered with spiked fingers and eyes.

"Gods?" Morgan asked Adonair. "Monsters?"

"I'm not sure."

Morgan asked Rayna, "Ever seen anything like these before?"

Rayna examined the statues with her light, while Morgan kept an eye out for intruders. "There are excavated ruins in the Sestian Republic with old statues like these," Rayna said. "I think they're supposed to be from the ancient Etolian age."

"Not a collection of local artworks based on the old stories?" Morgan asked. "That would seem more likely to me."

"That wouldn't make sense," Rayna said. "Why would modern statues be hidden in underground tunnels?"

"Not necessarily modern," Morgan said, "but not over a thousand years old, either. It's dry and dark here, good for storage and preservation."

"But look at this," Rayna said, pointing at an inscription hanging over a statue's three heads. "That's not Onglan."

Morgan turned to Adonair. "Volonian writing?"

After an awkward silence, Jairesse stepped forward. "It's an older script. There are many stories among our people about nonhuman and superhuman beings that inhabited our world long ago. After the eruption of the Great Nebula, much was destroyed, and valuable Volonian knowledge was lost during the dark age. There are some among us who dedicate their lives to theorizing and reconstructing what was but no longer is."

Morgan eyed Adonair, suspicious that he hadn't offered an explanation like Jairesse had. Leaving the ancient statues and proceeding deeper into the tunnels, he followed Rayna around a turn in the cave, passing the spot where Thakian had been killed.

"What do you think about…him?" Rayna asked Morgan in Alscrasian, her voice low, her head tilting toward Adonair.

"I'm keeping my eye on him," Morgan said. "Do you want to lead, while I bring up the rear?"

Rayna nodded, then paused. "One more thing— just to be clear—we are searching for the source of the particle beam."

"Yes."

"And when we run into Thakian's killer?"

"We defend ourselves." Morgan raised his gun.

"And your healer, too. I trust her. But keep your eye on our other friend." He felt a brief moment of anxiety over separating in the darkness, but it was the best way to maintain a defensive position in all directions.

"Got it."

Morgan drifted behind Adonair and Jairesse and pointed his light backward to confirm that they were alone.

They soon passed through an archway that opened into a circular cavern. Morgan stepped across a soft, carpet-like material that covered the floor in the deeper recesses of the cave. Although the ground cover exhibited the same blue-gray coloring as the surrounding rock, the texture differed. It was furry.

Rayna called from ahead, "Look at this."

She paused until Morgan and the others caught up. He shone his light on a dust-covered, rock-encrusted control console, thirty feet in height and width, built into the cavern's rock wall. Large gray tubes, emerging from the ground, entered the base of the console, rising through the top of the console along the wall. Morgan pointed his light upward, following the tubes up to the cavern ceiling, where they disappeared.

"Could be part of a massive construct," Morgan said. He knew that, during the golden age of Eurania, Onglus had been founded as a territorial outpost of the ancient Etolian Empire. If Jairesse's description of ancient lost knowledge was true, then it seemed possible that a powerful particle beam could have come from this location—given someone with the right knowledge to resurrect the machinery ruins. They could actually be pretty close to the source.

Rayna led the way forward, Adonair and Jairesse following, and Morgan bringing up the rear. Soon, they passed through a second archway that led out of the cavern and entered another passageway.

"Catacombs," Rayna said, pointing at more ruins lining the walls.

The passageway sloped upward. The right wall fell away, revealing a vast pit far below. Morgan picked up a fist-sized rock and tossed it over the edge. It bounced against the rock wall and plunged into the depths. Suddenly, a geyser of flame erupted from below. It vanished almost as quickly, leaving the echo of the blaze's roar vibrating through the cavern. A hint of sulfuric smoke drifted in the air.

Morgan began to piece together the image of a massive apparatus that drew unlimited power from the molten depths of Volon and channeled it up a tubular network, through an array of oversized transformer consoles similar to what they had passed.

The path continued to ascend, winding around the edge of the drop. Panning his light above, Morgan saw numerous overhanging boulders.

"Morgan!" Rayna called. She pointed up at a black shadow darting among the boulders.

Morgan tensed. Was it Thakian's killer?

Rayna panned her light along the rocky walls, unable to relocate the elusive figure. "I don't see how we can get up there without pulling down the boulders on top of ourselves."

"We need to be careful about this," Morgan said. "Maybe we can climb up farther ahead. Let me go first."

As he took a step up the path, a loud creak sounded from above.

"Move!" Rayna yelled at Adonair and Jairesse, the first few small pebbles tumbling down past them.

They charged ahead as an avalanche of rocks and boulders rained down where they had stood and bounded over the edge. The crashes and rattles reverberated for several more seconds after the last of the rubble disappeared into the void.

Morgan and Rayna snapped their lights up at a gaping hole in a line of overhead boulders and caught a brief glimpse of the black shadow dashing off behind a crevice in the wall. Rayna fired, the bright energy charge sailing through the hole and exploding in the distance with a loud concussion.

Lowering her gun, she said, "It's gone."

Morgan put a firm hand on Jairesse's shoulder. She was hyperventilating, clearly terrified, her eyes wide as they looked about. "Are you okay with continuing?" he asked her.

Jairesse took a moment to steady herself, then slowly nodded.

Rayna led the way forward again. But before they ventured much farther, the path stopped. Several feet ahead, across a short chasm, was another small opening and the beginning of another narrow tunnel, this one lined with two strings of small, bead-like green lights.

"It's only a few feet," Rayna said to Morgan. "We can jump it."

Morgan paused. "Are you sure, Rayna?" With a flicker of his eyes, he indicated Jairesse and Adonair.

Rayna glanced around, pointing her light first to the left along the jagged crevice, then to her right, straight down into the darkness, and finally up above. "There," she said, pointing at a short, raised bridge, "I'll bring it down."

"Be careful," Morgan said.

"Morgan, don't fuss."

She stepped away from the drop, waved Adonair and Jairesse aside, then motioned to Morgan to keep his light steady on the chasm.

Morgan gave the go-ahead and held his breath.

Rayna took a short running start and gracefully leaped over the chasm, landing with a few inches to spare. She ventured into the mouth of the tunnel, where she looked over a series of power panels and switches and a maze of colored lights.

She scanned her side of the chasm in all directions and, stepping out and away from the tunnel, disappeared behind a formation of boulders. "Here it comes," she called out.

The short bridge lowered, the lift mechanism creaking softly, unpowered. Morgan watched it settle into place, approving of Rayna's decision not to activate any of the machinery and avoiding the possibility of automated detection.

After they all crossed to the other side, Morgan and Rayna surveyed the new tunnel—a dirty pathway lined with the green bead-like lights and covered with metal plates, some translucent, others warped or cracked. It reminded Morgan of some of the access tubes on *Ocelot*. They followed it a short distance before Morgan stopped and pointed his light at a perpendicular crawlway, partially obscured by stones, that he noticed to his left.

"What do you think?" Morgan asked, pushing the larger stones aside to peer up the sloping crawlway.

"I've got a feeling," Rayna replied.

"Female intuition again?" Morgan asked.

Rayna smiled. "Have I been wrong yet?"

After shaking his head and conceding her point, Morgan examined the crawlway and saw that it was rough but empty.

"Let me lead," Rayna said.

Morgan nodded and stepped aside.

After she climbed in, Morgan helped Adonair

and Jairesse in. He made one last scan in all directions with his light, confirming that the shadowy figure was nowhere in the immediate vicinity, then entered the crawlway.

They inched their way along the claustrophobic tunnel, crawling on all fours over alloy tiles caked with dirt, an occasional dust cloud feathering over them when one of them brushed a loose outcropping. Morgan kept his eye out behind them, focusing on protecting everyone, and not on thoughts of being buried in a tunnel collapse.

After a long stretch of slithering over rounded and jagged rocks, and scraping through layers of dust and grit, Rayna came upon a small, closed access door at the end of the crawlway. She motioned for the others to stop. While they waited in silence, Morgan thought he detected a distant melody. Rayna gently pushed on the door and cracked it upward. A sliver of light entered the crawlway. While Morgan waited, she drew her gun and climbed out. A few seconds later, Rayna helped Adonair, Jairesse, and Morgan out.

They emerged among the desolate ruins of a shadowy, musty room. The strains of an out-of-tune flutelike instrument floated through the thick air. Morgan and Rayna swung their lights about, examining the surroundings. To one side of the room, near a closed door, sat a disordered arrangement of old mismatched furniture: a table, two chairs, and a standing lamp. A sagging wooden case holding disheveled piles of discs and ancient decrepit books lined another wall. Next to the case sat a small desk with a vintage video reader and a chair with reader controls on its arms. Large self-illuminated landscape pictures hung on the walls. A small control board, one of its small lights alternately blinking blue and green, lay in the far corner, obscured behind an electronic globe, adjacent to a set of closed double doors. Next to it, a low, narrow pass-through gave a view of an unlit connecting room.

The setting looked similar to a painting Moegan once saw of a simple Etolian-era parlor. He wondered what its original use might have been, and just how powerful were the ancient architects of this vast underground complex.

Turning to Jairesse, Adonair said, "The description in the Holy Book matches this room. I believe we have arrived."

Jairesse gave Morgan and Rayna a quick glance. "You will wait here." She removed her cape and handed it to Adonair. After a deep breath and a moment's hesitation, she opened the double doors and walked through, into a tunnel. A few seconds later, a flicker of light appeared from an inner chamber deep within the tunnel. A wisp of reddish-brown vapors drifted in from the tunnel.

"The Timegazer?" Morgan asked Adonair.

Adonair nodded.

"What's inside?" Rayna asked. The scent seemed an odd blend of seductive sweetness and repulsive stench.

"It is not for us to know," Adonair said. "Certainly not for those who are not even our own people."

Stonewalled again. Morgan debated whether to press the question. He didn't like Adonair. But Morgan trusted his instincts, and keeping Adonair engaged was the best way to keep an eye on the man,

He heard Jairesse begin a low, murmuring chant. "You understand what she's saying, don't you, Adonair?" Morgan asked.

Adonair glared at Morgan, then walked away.

Rayna walked over and asked Morgan, in Alscrasian, "What do you—?"

"Shh!" Morgan cut her off when the music stopped. "Move!"

They scrambled into hiding, Adonair back into the crawlway, Morgan and Rayna through the low pass-through into an adjoining compartment, a cluttered space filled with shelves of greasy machinery and tarnished tools. They shut off their lights, crouched, and listened.

Footsteps approached. A switch snapped, and a dim light illuminated the parlor. Morgan noticed a small, blurry but reflective metal box sitting on a low shelf within his reach. He quietly lifted it until he and Rayna could see through the pass-through on the metal's reflection.

A tall man appeared in the now-opened doorway, standing directly below a soft white light. The stranger seemed much taller than them, but otherwise looked human, with thin black hair and dark, beady eyes. He was dressed like an aristocratic gentleman from the Imperial worlds, in a white shirt, gray frock coat and trousers, and a small, golden disc in the middle of his shirt collar.

The gentleman gazed about the parlor. Morgan's fingers tightened around his gun. The man's eyes narrowed. Morgan tensed at the smile creeping into the stranger's face. The man quickly traversed the room and disappeared through the double doors.

Jairesse screamed.

Morgan and Rayna bounded out of the work room, passed through a short tunnel, and emerged into a large inner chamber, where they found Jairesse standing alone. Before her, the ruins of three earthen statues, all with their heads apparently broken off, were elevated on table-like pedestals along the back wall. Even without their heads, Morgan recognized the Three Guardians—the twin deities Cru and Thema, Guardians of the Past and Future, and Cqoeis, the Guardian of the Multiverse —from their birdlike wings and fishlike tails. A giant cauldron sat before the statues, odorous, red-brown smoke pouring out the top. Five-foot-tall flaming torches stood to either side of the statues, guarding two darkened exits. For an instant, Morgan thought he saw an image, something resembling a metropolis skyline with a hawklike shadow hovering over it, dissolving in the smoke. Jairesse had turned pale, and she shook uncontrollably. Rayna wrapped her arm around Jairesse's shoulder.

"Are you all right?" Morgan asked. He sneaked another quick glance at the cauldron, the smoke quickly fading away as Adonair entered the chamber.

Jairesse whispered, "His aura..."

"Who?" Rayna asked. "What did you feel?"

Jairesse withdrew from Rayna and turned away. "Foulness. Putridness." She stared at the floor. "There is a decaying rot surrounding him, a centuries-old aura of corruption."

"How can you sense this?" Morgan asked. "Who was that?"

Jairesse faced them. "In the same way that I am connected to the *Pankoulda*, he also is connected to the *Pankoulda*. In the same way that I am connected to Lord Oscanos and Mother Gheriah, he is connected to Luzomi."

"Luzomi?" Morgan asked. The name conjured an uneasy feeling.

Jairesse looked grim. "Luzomi, he who is—"

"Everybody knows," Morgan interrupted. "He's in those old tales of the Euranian Ancestors. He supposedly fought Oscanos for control of the human race in the primordial days of the universe."

"There are reportedly underground cults of

Luzomi scattered throughout Eurania," Rayna
added. "Whether Luzomi is real or not, I've heard
that his followers can be dangerous. Are you saying
this man is one of them?"

"He is not just a follower." Jairesse looked at
Rayna, then at Morgan. "He is receiving a
channeling of Luzomi's presence. At one time he
may have been human, but now he has become a
vehicle for Luzomi."

Morgan considered her words. This description
seemed too much like religious fanaticism for him
to consider seriously. The man had looked like an
ordinary gentleman. But Rayna's point about the
cults was legitimate.

"Do not dismiss Jairesse's warning," Adonair
said, raising his hands. "We are dealing with forces
beyond our own." He put his hands on Morgan and
Rayna's shoulders. "We do not know what will
become of this, if we provoke Luzomi. What dark
powers will enter into our lives?" He put his hands
together. "I appeal to you: heed Jairesse's warning.
Let us turn back."

Morgan didn't like the feel of this. More
importantly, he wondered if this mysterious person
could be connected to the particle beam. He made
eye contact with Rayna, unsure of how she felt
about venturing into what could turn into another
mystical experience. But when she drew her gun, he
knew she was ready to go. Turning to Adonair and
Jairesse, he said, "We're going after him."

Adonair wrapped his arm around Jairesse's shoulder. "I will take Jairesse back to the rover. We will wait for you there."

After assisting Jairesse and Adonair back into the crawlway and closing the access door behind them, Morgan and Rayna departed the inner chamber through one of the unlit doorways. Confronted with a long series of closed doors lining a darkened corridor, they explored slowly and carefully, opening several doors and peering inside.

"What do you think?" Rayna finally asked.

"This one." Morgan pointed at a doorway that led to an unlit ascending staircase. "Maybe this will take us to the top, where we can get a better view of this entire area."

They cautiously climbed a long circular staircase, eventually emerging into an observation room with a breathtaking view of the twin peaks through a translucent domed ceiling. One peak towered several hundred feet above them while the other rose high in the distance. In the far corner of the room, a small transparent door led outside onto the mountaintop.

A complex bank of tarnished instruments lined two walls of the room. At the intersection of the two long panels was a small seat, situated in front of a circular viewing screen and a set of controls. Directly above the viewing screen, two glowing yellow-and-orange energy tubes jutted out from the wall. The tubes ran parallel to the ceiling, one above each instrument panel, then turned down into the top of the machine at the two ends. A low hum droned from the machinery. In the opposite corner, partly hidden behind a scattering of portable equipment, was a partly open storage closet filled with coils, arrays, and a plethora of small transparent cases filled with jeweled crystals of different colors, shapes, and sizes.

Morgan said, excited, "Might this be the source of the particle beam?"

"But what is the particle beam?" Rayna asked.

Voices from outside interrupted them. Morgan and Rayna quickly stole away into the storage room and hid behind the equipment.

They spied from between two arrays of spare vintage power collectors and distributors as the transparent door swung open. The tall gentleman entered, now dressed in a long black cloak. Another man limped in, discarding a dented vest of armor and donning a hooded black robe. Morgan and Rayna exchanged looks when they recognized the limping man's bloodstained, dirt-covered face.

Adonair. Without Jairesse.

Why he was bloodied and disheveled, Morgan could only think the worst. Was Jairesse still alive? Was Adonair a prisoner?

"...your selfless dedication will be rewarded, my friend." The gentleman spoke Onglan with what sounded like an upper-crust Brozan accent.

Morgan froze. What was a Brozan doing on Volon? Broza currently held control of the Gearmlian Confederation, the largest and most militaristic constituent of the Central Empire. The Confederation was also nowhere near Volon. From the start, Morgan had felt uneasy about Adonair. Now he knew why the temple chief had acted so evasively. Had Adonair betrayed Jairesse?

"Do not worry about the intruders," the Brozan man continued.

"But, Mr. Saltos," Adonair said, "they are not like us. They are off-worlders."

"Off-worlders will not interfere with my plans." Saltos pointed at an arrangement of readouts on the panel. "I have repaired the traversal unit. The Timegazer will no longer rivet onto passing hyperspace ripples or currents." Saltos parted his lips, revealing short, yellow, sharpened incisors. "I will dispose of the two intruders already here, in my own time and means."

Adonair bowed his head. "I understand." He turned to the giant machine. "May I ask about this? I find it hard to comprehend that a scientific device, impressive as it may be, can reach into the realm of the spiritual."

"I have been slaving over this instrument for many, many decades," Saltos said. "Etolian script is not well understood. Without sufficient knowledge to repair the many worn and decayed components, the Timegazer sat in its own dust for centuries."

He swept his slender, bony hand toward the circular viewing screen, a grand gesture, and smiled.

"It is now in working condition and nearing final completion. I expect your assistance to prove most valuable. In its current state, there are many violent and uncontrolled effects." Saltos sat down in the control seat and activated the viewer. A pattern of spectrum waves appeared on the display, undulating like a school of sea snakes. "Watch the mountain peaks."

Morgan and Rayna peered toward the dome. A previously obscured disc, roughly ten feet in diameter and about one hundred feet above them on the peak, began emitting a whitish-yellow glow. A second disc, on the distant peak, also began glowing a soft yellow-and-orange light.

"When the underground accelerators power up," Saltos explained, "a chronon stream stretches between the two discs. I can focus a beam out into space, where it bursts open contact points between this universe and that of the ancient past." He switched off the viewer, and the glowing projectors faded. "Since my first successful test, I have been working on controlling the strength and duration of the contact points. They are weak and unstable, and the discharge is very violent."

"And the star medallion crystal?" Adonair asked.

"A powerful energy source," Saltos answered,

"able to transcend the spatial-temporal boundaries of this universe, if channeled properly."

Morgan and Rayna exchanged glances. Third-hand stories about the mysterious ways of the Luzomi cults, ranging from ritualistic animal sacrifices to barbaric human mutations, were prevalent. But neither had ever crossed paths with Luzomi followers before. At least, none that they were aware of. Given the secretive nature of the followers, it was not inconceivable for ordinary-looking commoners—like Saltos and Adonair—to be Luzomi worshippers.

Saltos held out his hand. Adonair reached into the folds of his robe and drew out a dull, charcoal-gray box. He opened it, and a bright golden gleam illuminated both of their faces.

"Beautiful." Saltos smiled, his lips parting to reveal his pointed fangs. He brought out a tiny green crystal and held it up to examine it. A strange golden shine glistened around it like a small halo.

"It was difficult keeping its discovery secret," Adonair said. "During the expedition, many people roamed through the caves, looking for all kinds of precious stones and metals. I had to go into hiding with this crystal." He bowed his head. "I humbly apologize for not delivering this sooner."

"You have atoned for your delay," Saltos pronounced. He eyed the crystal. "This priceless gem is exquisite." Lowering the crystal, he turned his chair to face the controls. "As a reward, you will receive a place of prominence in the court of Lord Luzomi." Saltos brushed his fingers over a relay of levers, tripping them. "Watch as I engage the time projector and receiver."

The power lines pulsed at a rapid rate into the machine. The low hum rose. A faint, high-pitched whistle sounded from above. Images of static bolts shot across the viewer, and the speaker crackled to life. Saltos turned down the room lights as a blur of light took form on the viewer.

"Behold the beauty of the fountain of eternal passage."

A twisted, rainbowlike beam projected from the near disc and stretched across the chasm to the far disc. Short, jagged energy bolts of different colors shot out in random directions from the beam and scattered over the atmosphere. Soft explosions sounded above the dome. The spiraling strands of energy coalesced into a shimmering field of light that climbed through the atmosphere, narrowing into a tight beam projected into the stratosphere.

Morgan and Rayna watched as the static web on the screen solidified into a shadowy scene of heavy activity below a metropolis skyline. Garbled sounds of mechanical noises and human voices grew discernible through the crackles. The scene reminded Morgan of some of the metropolises of the empire, though he didn't recognize this one.

The picture settled into a nighttime scene. Flying beings filled the skies, and panicked people scattered in all directions. In the distance, beyond the buildings, a monstrous horned, winged silhouette towered. Energy beams shot into the sky and arced down to the surface, touching off explosions and fires. Bloodred screaming bodies and flailing body parts hurtled through the air.

Rayna winced. Morgan clenched his hands. The images were of a human massacre by animalistic beings.

"Now, let us test this," Saltos said to Adonair.

Saltos stood up and opened a small light-lined drawer at the base of the energy tubes. He removed a ring with five large red crystals from the vessel and put it aside. He then took the green star medallion crystal, gave it one last examination, and inserted it into the vessel. Once connected, the interior of the compartment illuminated. Saltos closed the drawer, pushed it back into its housing, and returned to his seat. The activity of the giant machine increased noticeably. The energy tubes intensified their glow.

Morgan felt Rayna's hand on his arm. He nodded toward her, recalling the memories of the giant tubular construct and the flaming geysers they had encountered in the tunnels.

The images on the viewer sharpened. The energy beams that flew skyward on the viewer appeared to shoot out from a sea of raised arms. On the speaker, a loud roar erupted, drowning out all other sounds. A moment later, a whalelike silhouette entered into the picture, high above the city. Tiny swarms of blue light descended from the underside of the bulbous shadow and zipped down to the city streets. Mile-high explosions burst wherever the blue lights impacted the ground. Arches cracked; towers fell. Blood splattered throughout the scene as bodies burst and collapsed in the street. Dark clouds rolled through the skies, obscuring the stars.

Morgan recognized what the images were depicting—the stories of the mythical war among the Euranian Ancestors—and wondered if that was what he had seen earlier in the smoke pouring out of the cauldron.

Saltos changed the display to show columns of numbers. "We have some contact points emerging." He changed the display again, and a second list of numbers began scrolling down. He frowned. "Most are unstable and closing already." He studied the numbers, then pointed to several. "Yes, we have a few perpetual points."

Adonair smiled, rubbing his hands together.

Morgan pointed out the rainbow to Rayna, its skyward beam achieving a tighter focus. A green tint shaded the edge of the rainbow. The beam developed a whirling, twisting movement, and the bolts that shot out from the beam turned to predominantly blinding pink and a light shade of gray.

"That's it," Morgan whispered to Rayna. They had found the particle beam that had shot them down. It had been fired from some sort of gargantuan space-time-transcending machine, under the control of a Luzomi worshipper.

"We have success," Saltos said. "It is nearly complete." He disengaged the power, and the rainbow dissipated. The picture froze. The echoes of the ancient destruction faded, and the ghostlike images on the viewer dissolved. Saltos turned to Adonair. "You should begin preparations for the sacrifice. The time is upon us to welcome Lord Luzomi into our midst."

Saltos rose from the chair and, with Adonair, departed down the stairs back to the parlor, leaving Morgan and Rayna to contemplate what they had witnessed, and what to do next.

3. Image of Luzomi

Morgan stared at the monstrosity of machinery that dominated the observation room. He held his breath. His muscles tensed. The network of energy tubes extended upward like rising tentacles. The oversized circular viewer was like a glass eye. This was what had shot them down and almost killed Rayna.

It didn't matter that it hadn't been Saltos's intention to shoot them down. Apparently, the particle beam wasn't supposed to lock onto their passing spacecraft, nor even cross from normal space into hyperspace. It didn't matter that they were just in the wrong place at the wrong time.

Even though this was an ancient scientific marvel, it was also a deadly menace. Rayna had almost lost her life. The next shot into space could strike another passerby—one less fortunate than Rayna had been. It had to be disabled.

Rayna asked, "Do you understand what just happened?"

Morgan shook his head. "Not totally. We need to get Adonair. We know he's a traitor to his own people."

She nodded. "We can get some answers out of him."

They dove down the flights of stairs, reentered the deserted inner sanctuary, and slowed upon hearing the soft shuffling of footsteps. Morgan and Rayna quickly slipped back into the darkened passageway. Crouching out of sight, they waited.

The footsteps paused. A low scratching noise sounded for a few seconds. Then, more footsteps, followed by a grunt, a heavy thud, and hammering. After a short pause, the footsteps returned, and the sequence repeated. They continued waiting, Morgan listening for any change in the sequence of sounds as they repeated a third time. His muscles tensed, ready to spring. Rayna remained motionless. Was it Adonair or the mysterious Saltos?

The footsteps faded away. Except for the crackling flames of the torches, the chamber went quiet. Cautiously, Morgan and Rayna peered in. Three tall wooden poles had been erected, arranged in a semicircle on the side of the room opposite the statues of the Three Guardians.

Adonair backed into the room, dragging a fourth pole along the ground.

Perfect.

Adonair, standing only a few feet away, pushed the wooden post upright, completing the arrangement of poles. As Adonair began hammering wedges into its base, Morgan holstered his pistol and silently unsheathed one of his skiloblades. Rayna also brought out one of her skiloblades. Morgan pointed into the chamber, and she flung her blade across the room, the metallic weapon bouncing off the far wall with a soft clang. Adonair turned, startled, and Morgan exploded into the chamber. He gripped Adonair's mouth with his free hand and yanked Adonair backward until he was pressed tight against Morgan's chest.

"Don't make a sound," Morgan whispered, the two sharp points of the skiloblade pressing into Adonair's neck. "We don't want to hurt you. Do you understand?"

Adonair, his eyes bulging, nodded.

Morgan released one finger after another from Adonair's mouth and moved his grip along Adonair's collar until he held the back of the man's hood, leaving Adonair free to take a long, slow breath.

"What's that machine upstairs?" Rayna asked, stepping out to retrieve her blade. "And what did you do with Jairesse?"

"I don't know where she is," Adonair whimpered. "I left her in the tunnels."

"How?" Rayna asked.

"I took a fall to fake my death."

"That's why you're all bloody like *shat'oq*?" Morgan asked, incredulous. He wanted to know more about the fake death, but there were more pressing questions to ask. "Who's the other man?"

"Saltos, my master." Tears welled in Adonair's eyes. "Please, I only do as I am told."

"Why are you working for him?" Rayna asked. "How are you involved in all this?"

"Please, no." A tear rolled down Adonair's face.

"Don't stall!" Morgan snapped his head about, in case Saltos reappeared without warning. There were too many questions—the machine's purpose, the nature of the images they saw, who Saltos was. Who Adonair really was, for that matter. Morgan tightened his grip and gave the hood's collar a sharp twist, choking Adonair. "Answer her."

"I'll tell what I know," Adonair wheezed, as Morgan relaxed his grip. "But believe me, I honestly don't know much."

"Explain why a temple chief like you is a follower of Luzomi."

"Luzomi is our creator," Adonair said, "our true lord."

"You're a traitor to your people," Morgan said. "And to Jairesse."

Adonair flung a crazed gaze at the three headless statues. "If you knew the inner workings of the temple like I do, you would know that the institutional worship of the *Pankoulda* is corrupted." He swallowed, the light from the torches dancing across his face. "Mr. Saltos is a priest of Luzomi. He has a clear understanding of the ways of our creator, what is required, what is desired."

The guy talks like a crazy fanatic, Morgan thought, *like a cult follower.* Even though he didn't believe in the stories of the Euranian Ancestors, Morgan knew enough to understand that Adonair had reversed the traditional interpretation of those stories. Morgan switched tactics, hoping to get some useful information. "What is that machine upstairs?"

"I don't know."

Dox! This was taking too long. Morgan and Rayna probably knew as much about the Timegazer as Adonair did.

"What are you working on," Rayna asked, "now that you've delivered your crystal?"

"A perfect offering. With the means to welcome Luzomi into our universe, we can usher a new age to our present reality." Adonair smiled, another tear rolling down his cheek.

"You're *kroking* crazy!" Morgan snapped.

Rayna asked, "Who are you sacrificing, and what's the connection with that particle beam?"

Adonair stiffened and gave no answer.

They turned at the sound of approaching footsteps. Morgan muffled a curse and pulled Adonair back outside, through the connecting tunnel to the parlor. After giving Adonair a warning gesture with his skiloblade, Morgan motioned for Rayna to stand ready on one side of the double doors while he took the other side. Once in position, he replaced his skiloblade and readied his gun. Rayna stood ready with hers. Adonair, tears streaming down his face, backed step by step past the closed crawlway hatch, toward the opposite doorway.

The footsteps stopped. Morgan, with the tension of the moment getting on his nerves, felt certain that Saltos knew they were there. He resisted his instinct to jump out in front of the double doors and face his target. Instead, he glanced at Adonair, and for an instant, Morgan felt sorry for the clearly confused Volonian.

Without warning, a pair of bony hands appeared in the opposite doorway and, with a quick flip of the wrists, whipped a length of rope over Adonair's head, tightening it about his neck until Adonair winced from the strain. A black cloth immediately smothered Adonair's head and yanked him backward through the opening.

"Adonair!" Morgan charged after Adonair, Rayna hot on his heels. But a second before they reached the doorway, unseen trips snapped. Morgan and Rayna barely leaped back before metal bars slammed down over the doorway, the small access door, and the double doors, sealing them within the parlor.

A scream echoed throughout the halls, into the parlor.

"Jairesse," Rayna whispered.

"*Krok!*" Morgan cursed, slamming his fist against one of the bars. The loud clang echoed through the parlor. He took out one of his skiloblades, released the duo-blades, and tapped it against one of the bars, producing a tinny ping. He then placed the edge against the bar, made a hard, sharp slice, and examined the cut. Nothing.

"Let me try," Rayna said.

She twisted a small dial on the top of her charge-lock gun, pointed it at the bar, and squeezed the trigger. A tight, narrow shot exploded against the bar.

Morgan examined the bar. Still nothing. This alloy was stubborn.

Rayna fired again, this time holding the trigger down so that the gun rapid-fired at the bar. Explosions burst at the point of contact. White smoke poured out. The bar quickly changed from its gray metallic color to bright white.

"Let's take a look," Morgan said, holding up his hand.

Rayna let up, and after the bar faded back to gray, Morgan examined it. He ran his hand up and down the bar, feeling for any change or scarring. Again, nothing. *Dox!* As Rayna reholstered her gun, Morgan scanned the room.

"There's got to be a release somewhere." He tried the controls in the reader chair, but only managed to activate the old video reader. They checked the control console in the corner. Several of the switches lit the electronic globe with different lights; others dimmed or brightened the overhead lights. One controlled the lights that illuminated the artwork on the wall.

Rayna folded her arms in frustration. "He's sacrificing Jairesse, isn't he?"

Somehow, they had stumbled into the midst of a religious conflict. Morgan took out his gun. "Double the power."

They fired simultaneously at the bar, drawing more blasts and smoke. The bar quickly returned to its white-hot appearance. Morgan could tell that, despite the searing energy cascading against it, the bar was still intact. His frustration mounting, he switched his gun to his off hand and, while maintaining a steady fire on the bar, brought his skiloblade back out with his free hand. He eyed the spot being pounded by the two sidearms, raised his blade, and swung as hard as he could. The skiloblade hit with a shower of sparks and a powerful blast that threw Morgan backward onto the ground.

"Morgan!" Rayna ran over to where Morgan lay.

Coughing, he tried to sit up, but collapsed back down. "Agh," he groaned. "That was brilliant."

"Don't try anything like that again," Rayna scolded. "Are you hurt?"

Morgan shook his head clear. "I'm all right."

Rayna picked up the seared skiloblade handle

stub and showed it to Morgan. The duo-blades had vaporized, the end of the handle stub melted. He sucked his breath in. It could have been his hand or his arm. Or his whole body.

A laugh sounded.

Morgan and Rayna pivoted around to face Saltos, standing in the tunnel on the other side of the bars. His rage erupting at the sight of the mysterious man, Morgan charged and reached through the bars to grab Saltos.

Saltos gave Morgan's hand a sharp slap.

"Ah!" Morgan held his hand until the pain subsided. Three ragged scratches ran across his knuckles. "*Turkanaan!*"

Saltos merely smiled at Morgan's curse.

Rayna pointed her gun at Saltos. "Let us go!"

"Kill me, and you shall remain trapped in there for the rest of your mortal lives," Saltos declared. He chuckled again, baring his incisors and rubbing his hands together.

"*Krok.*" Morgan struggled to contain his anger. Rayna had a clear shot at Saltos, but Morgan knew that Saltos was right—killing him wouldn't help them get out. Morgan took a deep breath to steady himself and try a different tactic. "Why are you sacrificing Jairesse to Luzomi?"

"She is the perfect offering for my master," Saltos said, "and she walked right into my parlor, of her own accord, thanks to your protective escort."

Morgan muffled a curse. Saltos—whoever he

was—was sly, manipulative, and crazed. What was truth, and what was deception? "*Where* is Luzomi?" Morgan asked. While the activities of Saltos, Adonair, and the giant machine were very real, Luzomi was just a figure in a story.

"He will be arriving soon." With that, Saltos stepped away.

Rayna looked to Morgan for the order to fire.

Morgan shook his head. They still had to figure out how to get out before they could tackle Saltos and find out who, exactly, "Luzomi" was.

Jairesse screamed again from the other end of the tunnel, and a heavy metal door slammed shut, the concussion echoing through the tunnel.

"Jairesse!" Rayna called out.

Morgan, holding up his hand to silence Rayna, thrust his gun into her hand. He had an idea, but with Saltos in the vicinity, they had to work quietly. Morgan detached the empty skiloblade sheath from his vest, released the small oval cartridge from his gun barrel, and squeezed the charge-pak inside the empty sheath.

Morgan then pointed at Rayna's gun.

She gave him a questioning look. When she realized he was referring to her charge-pak, she mouthed, "Not mine, too?"

Morgan nodded. He knew he was blowing both of their firearms, but he had to make sure this was going to work. They had only one shot at this.

She drew in her breath, took Morgan's sheath,

released her charge-pak, and added it to the bundle.

Morgan then detached his remaining sheath from his vest, sliced it open with his blade, and used it to tie the charge-pak bundle in place around the bar. After shaping the bundle with his fingers so that the two charge-paks bulged out together through the sheath, he whispered, "Not pretty."

Rayna cautioned, "I hope you know what you're doing."

"Me too." He gave her a quick, firm squeeze on her shoulder. He knew she was good at target practice; he hoped she would be just as good in a real-life situation.

They overturned the table and crouched behind it. Morgan nodded, and Rayna took out one of her skiloblades.

She released the duo-blade, took a deep breath to relax herself, peeked out from behind the table, and took aim. With blinding speed, she whipped the blade toward the bundle. A split second later, the two punctured charge-paks exploded, the two concussions rocking the room. The air filled with searing heat and suffocating smoke. Shrapnel rained down around them. After the cascade passed, Morgan and Rayna emerged from behind the debris-pelted table.

A large section of the bars gaped open.

As Morgan and Rayna squeezed through the hole in the bars, another scream sounded. They took out their remaining skiloblades and followed the scream down the short tunnel to the solitary, unmarked door, now closed.

Yet another scream.

Then, a low roar.

Morgan tried to kick the door open. Another scream sounded from inside. Frustrated, he pounded the door with his fist. Unable to budge it, he rested his head against it and tried to think of another way, his heart racing, his muscles tight with tension. He realized there must have been something holding the door in place. He raised his head and took a close look at the top edge of the door. Then he saw it: the track of the door. He inserted his skiloblade into the upper track and slid it until he tripped the lock.

The door swung open with a loud creak. Morgan switched on his light, revealing a squat green candle in the center of the room, still burning, a faint stench drifting in the stale air.

Swinging his light to one side of the room, he saw the statues of the Three Guardians with the extinguished torches on either side. Before the statues stood the cauldron, no longer smoldering, and an eight-foot-high earthen figure of a bipedal reptilian creature.

Morgan swung his light to the other side of the room and saw the four wooden poles. Adonair hung from one pole, limp and blindfolded. Jairesse hung from a second, her robe torn to tatters.

"*Krok!*" Morgan yelled as he and Rayna dashed

to Jairesse.

Rayna placed her hand on Jairesse's shoulder and tried to rouse her. "She's still breathing," Rayna said to Morgan with a hint of hope.

Jairesse could not lift her head or open her eyes. But she could whisper. "...Prince..." She paused, her breathing difficult. "...of Evil..."

Morgan and Rayna listened, but Jairesse spoke no further.

"Stay with us," Rayna coaxed.

Morgan untied Jairesse and, as gently as he could, lowered her to the ground. They watched her to ascertain that she still breathed, though the breaths were slow and shallow. Morgan took off his jacket and covered her.

Rayna removed her jacket and placed it under Jairesse's head, cushioning it from the cold, hard ground. "She saved me," she whispered.

Morgan, trying to focus on their situation, stepped away and shone his light on Adonair. "Oh God." Adonair was not breathing. What Morgan could see of Adonair's face was as pale as a ghost. Morgan removed the black blindfold, studied Adonair's face, and felt his neck for a pulse. "Adonair's dead."

"Just like Thakian," Rayna whispered, grim.

Morgan had never liked Adonair, but he still felt sad for him. Morgan froze as he realized that the two empty poles might have been intended for himself and Rayna.

He turned to face the strange statue. It looked like a dinosaur with butterfly wings and oversized goat horns. He remembered frightening pictures from his childhood lessons of this beast, scenes of it and other giant creatures terrorizing crowds of people. In one particularly memorable image he once saw in a library, it was stomping across a hillside, trampling through people and animals, with a naked woman in its claw and a bloody, half-eaten man in its mouth. "This is Luzomi, isn't it?"

"I think you're right," Rayna said. "I never thought I would see this in real life."

Morgan stepped around it and looked it over. "It's just an earthen statue, like the others."

"He has the power to give life," said a low voice from the mouth of the tunnel, "or to take life."

Morgan whirled about and shone the light on Saltos.

Rayna demanded, "What did you do to her?" She raised her skiloblade and charged.

"Rayna—no!" Morgan yelled.

Saltos suddenly jumped high into the air, flying directly at Rayna, his cloak flaring like large black wings. Startled, Rayna took a quick step aside. Saltos landed with a bound and jump-kicked his legs into her stomach, knocking her to the wall with a blow so jarring that her skiloblade dislodged from her hand and fell to the ground. She gasped, out of breath and wincing from the pain of the blow, her arms wrapped about her abdomen.

Morgan froze for a second with the memory of Rayna lying unconscious in the forest before he turned his head to see Saltos charge. On reflex, he raised his blade and lunged at the approaching Saltos. But just as Morgan was about to strike, Saltos hurtled high over Morgan and descended upon Rayna. Off-balance, Morgan spun about, too late to defend her.

Rayna managed to roll aside, avoiding Saltos's downward strike. She swung a powerful blow into Saltos's head, knocking him back enough to give her an opening. She grabbed her blade and scrambled away on all fours into the corner.

Saltos spun around to face Morgan, his eyes now glowing an eerie green, his fangs protruding. "Behold," Saltos proclaimed, "the lord of the human race arrives!"

Morgan swung around to see the statue emit a glowing gray-green misty cloud into the air, directly above its head. Small puffs of pink-and-gray light appeared around the cloud. The wings swayed, folding and unfolding. Its tongue slithered in and out of its gaping mouth. Its tail swung back and forth like a giant serpent. The claws of its tiny forearms flexed, opening and closing. A red pinpoint sparkle radiated within the medallion that hung from its neck. Within seconds, a rainbow of tiny twinkles covered the jeweled surface of the medallion. The golden-green eyes of Luzomi blinked.

4. *The Xaturi's Howl*

Morgan didn't have time to think. Lightning bolts crackled from the shimmering multicolored cloud, covering the statue in a web of static electricity, transforming its surface from earthen clay to thick, scaly skin. He raised his twin-shaft skiloblade and charged the statue of Luzomi.

Saltos screamed.

Morgan swung as hard as he could, hacking into the statue's head. A blinding flash of light, an explosive burst of smoke, and a blast of energy destroyed Morgan's remaining blade and threw him, Rayna, and Saltos off their feet. The ceiling cracked, and the statue's medallion went flying into the corner. Morgan crashed into one of the poles. A jolt of excruciating pain shot from his ribs into his spine, radiating outward to his limbs. He struggled to regain his senses and clear his head.

The statue, headless and with thick black smoke

pouring out of a gaping hole in its neck, toppled over and crashed to the floor, shattering into a thick blanket of dust and debris. As the multicolored cloud disappeared, a demonic cry echoed like the flapping of giant wings. The overpowering stench of pomira bark smothered the air.

Morgan felt a cold tentacle brush his body. Rayna, pushing herself off the ground, drew back and whirled about, as if startled by an invisible presence enveloping her. Then the rush of air from the blast died, and the howl blended into Saltos's cry.

Saltos raised his hands into the air, his shirt darkening to a charcoal-gray fur, his cloak unfolding and transforming into real wings of black, leathery skin. His arms bent at an awkward angle to become foreclaws. Saltos's clean-shaven face darkened into a rough, blackish visage, framed by uneven tufts of black hair and pointed sideburns. His eyebrows lengthened and thickened, sweeping over his slit-like green eyes. His nose hooked like a beak, and two long fangs extended from the row of upper incisors, descending out of his open mouth. A black, lizard-like tongue slithered in and out. Tiny brown horns rose from his scalp. The gold disc in the collar of his black cloak glowed.

The creature spread its wings and dove into Morgan. Morgan spun, sidestepping it. He swung his fist at the creature but missed. The black being landed on its feet and howled at Morgan, its incisors bared.

From her corner, Rayna charged at it. She swung her blade and swiped it in the arm, drawing a loud cry and a gush of green, oozing blood. She stumbled past the fallen statue, into the opposite corner of the room, and grabbed the still-lit medallion.

Morgan thought he could still recognize Saltos's distorted facial features within the black being's visage. "Are you Saltos or the Xaturi?"

The creature hissed and turned to face him. Holding its wounded arm, it said in a low, rumbling tone, "We are one."

A hybrid creature? Morgan took a quick glance at Jairesse, lying on the ground. She was unconscious but still alive, her chest rising and falling with shallow breaths. He made eye contact with Rayna, who was still holding the medallion out toward the Xaturi.

It suddenly whirled and extended its foreclaw toward Rayna. "Give!" It charged at her, its wings extended. She quickly tossed the medallion past the Xaturi's reach. The Xaturi howled and dove for the medallion, but the object sailed inches beyond its grasp into Morgan's hand.

The Xaturi raged with fury. There was something about this medallion, Morgan knew, something this creature wanted or needed. It had killed before to get it, and it would kill again.

Rayna dashed past the Xaturi, toward Jairesse. It

ignored her and charged him. Morgan tensed, his breath drawn to steel himself against the pain, his fists cocked. But as it came upon him, Rayna whipped her remaining blade through the air, sinking it deep into its back.

The Xaturi cried out and crashed to the ground, the hilt protruding from the base of its neck. Relentless, it rebounded, its wings thrusting it upward from what should have been a fatal blow.

Rayna was now completely weaponless. Morgan had only one course of action that would protect her. He dangled the medallion before the Xaturi, then turned away and ran out of the inner chamber, the roaring Xaturi in hot pursuit.

Ignoring the shot of pain that erupted with each step, he mounted the staircase and burst into the observation room. He ran past the control seat, the banks of instruments, and the giant energy tubes, and out the side door.

On the mountaintop, a gust of cold wind blasted him, blowing him off his feet. Regaining his balance, Morgan wheeled around to survey his surroundings. Overhead, dark clouds swirled in the turbulent air. Deep-red rays from the rising sun gave the clouds an explosive, angry quality. Rumblings echoed throughout, and intermittent flashes illuminated the chasms. Large boulders, some jagged and black, others rounded and silver, dotted the blue ash that smoothed the surface of the mountain. A blue path, winding between some of the boulders, sloped up and away.

Perhaps it leads to the near projector disc. As he climbed the rocks, he kept glancing back to watch for the Xaturi. He paused when he reached a clearing formed by a circle of jagged boulders towering over him.

The path ahead narrowed to a short bridge that stretched over a crevasse between two sheer walls. Below, a layer of dark clouds swirled, concealing the depths of the crevasse. The wind raced through the corridor with a tremendous fury, buffeting both walls with blue ash. A bolt of lightning shot down from the overhead clouds into the heart of the chasm. The lower clouds blinked a soft orange glow. A muffled concussion echoed along the mountain walls.

Morgan took a deep breath and stepped onto the bridge. Halfway across, the bridge narrowed to less than five feet in width. A sudden gust of wind nearly blew him over. Pausing to regain his balance, he caught a glance of the precipitous drop through a break in the clouds below him. Not far above, lightning crackled through the dark clouds. Morgan could feel the static in his hair. Another lightning bolt flashed in front of him, striking the bridge with a glancing blow. The booming thunderclap pounded his ears. Determined, Morgan charged ahead.

Once on the other side, the steep slope wound around a giant rock formation. He found himself standing about fifty feet below the circular projector disc. He walked around it, studying the backside components that rose from the ground. There seemed to be a bundle of energy conduits that went into a transformer before connecting to the back of the disc.

Morgan jumped, startled by a lightning bolt flashing down into the drop. When he gathered himself, he saw a tall black figure descend in front of him. Morgan snapped into a defensive posture as the Xaturi stepped forward.

"Do not run!" Its voice echoed into the wind. It extended its foreclaw. "I am only my master's slave, serving his purposes. Do not fear me. I am condemned and am more a victim than those who have died at my hands."

Jairesse had said that Saltos had once been human but was now a vehicle for Luzomi. Was this creature speaking the truth about its nature?

"I am compelled to shed blood for my master's rule. Have mercy for a tortured soul."

Morgan tensed his jaw, his resolve stiffened. "You serve a liar, and you are a liar yourself. You ask for mercy, yet how many of your victims asked you for mercy?"

"If you must destroy me," it replied, "do so out of pity, not vengeance. Killing me would set me free."

Morgan gritted his teeth. He would kill it—but how? With rocks? Morgan held up the medallion. "Is this what you want?" He would bait it. "Would it have brought that statue to life?"

It took another step forward, its wings folding. "It is one of the ancient crystals that Lord Luzomi gave to us in former times, with the ability to tap its primordial power to further his aims."

"You used Adonair's crystal to power your machine. How many of these crystals are there?"

It held out its foreclaws. "Nobody knows, except Lord Luzomi himself."

"What did that machine do when you fired the particle beam?"

"Enough!" the Xaturi interrupted. "My master awaits the sacrifice that will unlock the door to his entrance."

Morgan kept his guard up, gauging the space between himself and the approaching Xaturi. He eyed the medallion. "Luzomi's entrance…with this?" It seemed the crystals—both Adonair's and the one embedded in this medallion—were key to this creature's aims. Morgan took a step back.

"It is mine," it roared. "It is of no use to you."

The Xaturi took another step toward Morgan, its arm outstretched. Keeping his eye on his opponent, Morgan knelt down and placed the medallion on the ground.

"No!" the Xaturi cried.

In one swift motion, Morgan grabbed a jagged black stone and brought it down on the medallion with all his might. The concussion rocked the area, the medallion disintegrating in a shower of light and sparks, shrapnel from the stone flying in all directions. The explosion blew Morgan toward the bridge, and he crashed to the ground onto his already bruised back.

Morgan fought against the pain and scrambled to his knees. Another lightning bolt lit up the sky. A faint groan and rot-like breath alerted him. He spun around just as it rushed him from behind. Roaring a monstrous cry, it butted its horns into his chest. Morgan's world turned upside down, and he crashed to the ground under the weight of the lunging creature, stunned by the pain in his back.

It thrust both foreclaws under Morgan and scooped him up, its wings extending to lift Morgan into the air. Realizing that the creature intended to throw him over the cliff, Morgan flailed his arms and legs about, helpless. He yanked his torso away, and the Xaturi lost its balance, crashing to the ground on top of Morgan, the blow punching into his abdomen.

Pinned at the edge of the bridge, Morgan struggled to roll away. The creature's leathery wings fell over his face, blinding him for a moment and smothering him in its stench. His legs free, Morgan kicked into its back with all his strength and, in one motion, rolled the creature under him. It roared and shot its scaly, forked tongue out at him, barely missing Morgan's eyes as he dodged to one side. With a split-second clear line of sight, Morgan shot his fist into its head, scoring a full-force strike between the eyes, stunning it.

Morgan scrambled to his feet, his hand throbbing from delivering the hit. As it regained its legs, Morgan booted a powerful kick into its head, sending it crashing to the ground with a cry of pain. With lightning quickness, he seized both claws and dragged the creature, like a heavy burden, back toward the edge of the cliff.

Regaining its senses, it planted a foothold and dove straight into him, slamming into his stomach, horns first, knocking Morgan's breath out. They both crashed to the ground, Morgan's head dangling over the cliff as a bolt of lightning shot into the crevasse. Morgan saw two balls of static electricity flash before his eyes. The Xaturi's glowing hands reached for Morgan's face.

This is how it killed Thakian and Adonair!

Morgan summoned all his remaining energy to deliver a bone-cracking kick to the side of its abdomen, drawing a spew of blood from its mouth as it fell over the edge, screaming. Morgan caught a brief glimpse of it disappearing into the clouds below.

Trembling, struggling to breathe, Morgan waited until the cold wind numbed the waves of pain. He rolled to his feet and staggered across the bridge to the dome of the observation room. Peering inside, he saw Rayna crouched by the control seat with her arm over her abdomen. She waved her free hand to him. He smiled, exhausted, and started back toward the control room's side door. But before he took his second step, he heard an ear-piercing howl from behind.

It was the Xaturi, reappearing out of the crevasse with its giant wings flapping. Its voice screaming at the top of its lungs, it soared high above the bridge.

Sheer terror engulfed Morgan as it banked and dove toward him, its bloody, incisor-lined mouth gaping open. He sprinted for the door, the shadow of the Xaturi looming large over him. Feeling the rush of air from its flapping wings, he doubled back, just as its talons swooped over his head. Now cut off from the door, he scrambled back across the bridge, looking madly for a rock or anything else that he could use against it. He saw a pulsating light and sprinted for it. He heard another roar as he rounded a boulder and ran past the glowing time-projector disc.

A sudden gust of wind blew, and the Xaturi's roar became a scream. Morgan looked back to see a twisted rainbow beam spiral out from the now-activated projector disc. Hurricane winds rushed through the chasm, slamming Morgan against the mountain wall. The ground shook with violent tremors. An ear-piercing howl drowned out the cascade of thunderclaps that accompanied the onslaught of lightning bolts rocketing between the cloud banks.

The particle beam enveloped the Xaturi in mid-flight, blanketing the creature in a bath of twisting colors. It cried out and burst into flames as it fought to free itself of the time distortion. Flailing its wings, it shredded itself into fine, burning cinder-like tatters of flesh and skin. On the other peak, the receiver disc blazed a blinding white, then exploded into an earth-shattering blast of energy, a dark-gray smoke cloud rising from it.

Morgan collapsed to the ground, battered by the blast. Everything came to a stop—the tremor, the high-pitched wind, the temporal beam, the dying scream of the Xaturi. Looking into the sky, Morgan saw a mist of thin, flaming remnants float down through the breeze. Above, the soft rumblings and occasional lightning flashes continued.

Rayna, staggering across the bridge, embraced Morgan. "Are you all right?"

Ignoring the pain in his back, he wrapped his sweat-drenched arms around her. "Are you?" Of all the things he admired about her, he was most grateful, at this moment, that they had been of one mind during their fight to the death. Their instinct to turn the particle beam against the Xaturi had destroyed the creature. He whispered, exhausted, "You're a lifesaver."

"I thought I'd lost you." Rayna buried her head in his shoulder. "I'm just glad it's dead."

Morgan gazed over at the other peak, where a flaming cloud of smoke and ash rose high into the stratosphere like an erupting volcano. "Good riddance, Luzomi."

Morgan and Rayna stared at the mammoth machinery—the now dead and silent Timegazer. The energy tubes sat dark. The view screen was blank. The controls that Rayna had worked, just minutes before, sat lifeless.

"Whatever it was," Morgan said, "it won't be shooting any more particle beams through space. At least we accomplished that much."

They supported each other down the long staircase, back into the dark inner sanctum. There, Jairesse lay at the feet of the Three Guardians, still unconscious, but breathing. Rayna knelt and took her hand, checking her pulse, while Morgan released Adonair's body from the pole and gently lowered it to the ground.

"How are we going to get her back to the rover?" Rayna asked.

Morgan sighed. He was drained, but they needed to get Jairesse back to her people. Hopefully, other Volonians could help revive her, as Jairesse had revived Rayna. He went back to Adonair's body, whispered, "Sorry," and removed Adonair's robe. "This will help us carry her out." After crossing Adonair's arms over his chest, similar to how Jairesse had crossed Thakian's arms, Morgan spread the robe out on the ground next to Jairesse, and together they lifted her and placed her on the robe. Morgan paused, flinching at the painful bruises in his ribs and back, and asked, "Do you think you're up to it?"

Rayna tilted her head at Morgan and sighed. "Do you really need to ask?"

Epilogue

Morgan and Rayna, standing outside the Buggy, watched the four Volonian rovers depart the clearing. The dawn of the new day shone down over the forest. Inside one of the vehicles, Jairesse remained unconscious. Morgan felt bad for the Volonians who, upon seeing the titanic explosion on the mountain, had come in search of Jairesse, Adonair, and Thakian. A contingent of *Illito* warriors cried out when Morgan told them of Thakian's death. A second group, clerics from the temple, were stunned speechless at the news of Adonair's betrayal. All were sorrowful to the point of despondency upon learning of Jairesse's condition.

Only the priestess could perform a revival, they told Morgan and Rayna. A young novice had begun her training, but given her young age, it would be years—perhaps decades—before she would have mastered the ability without Jairesse's guidance. Whether Jairesse could be kept alive until then, no one knew.

Jairesse's condition also meant that no one would know whether the appearance of the *Hruvrah* truly marked the beginning of a period of turmoil and conflict unseen since the mythical age.

Upon reentering the ruined Buggy, Morgan pointed at the message displayed on the console comm monitor. "Look, Rayna, a rescue craft has been dispatched."

"What a relief," Rayna said.

Morgan gazed out the window, waiting until the sounds of the rovers had faded away into the distance. Part of him wanted to return, sometime in the future, to check on Jairesse. But part of him also wanted to leave this world of glowing hands, floating bodies, and Luzomi creatures behind—forever.

Rayna rubbed his shoulder, interrupting his musings. "We should get our belongings. The rescue craft will be arriving soon."

Morgan sighed. There was always something else to take care of. "Let me put out a response first." He sat in the pilot's seat and switched on the transmitter.

"Space Fortress C, this is *BG-832*, on the surface of Volon, Lieutenant Teggo speaking. Please advise the base commander that the source of the particle beam has been neutralized. We will be filing our reports with Captain Choff and Captain Jaron upon our return. Teggo out."

Mindful of his back and rib injuries, Morgan leaned back in his chair and placed his hands on the armrests. Rayna sat next to him, quiet. They had a couple hours alone now. The near loss of Rayna had made Morgan realize that nothing in life could be taken for granted.

He reached over and took her hand. "We won't make it to Toutle this time, but we still have our future to consider. I don't want to wait until we have another opportunity to go on leave together. I..."

It was hard to say the words. Rayna gave his hand a gentle squeeze.

"I almost lost you." Morgan's voice cracked, and he struggled to keep his composure.

Rayna's eyes were moist. "I almost lost you, too."

Morgan took a deep breath. "We both know that anything can happen, at any time. But we've never actually gone through anything like this before, putting our lives on the line."

"It wasn't just another academy exercise, was it?"

Morgan hesitated. He knew he wasn't eloquent; he could only hope that she would understand what he intended to express. "I learned something important: you and I have something ethereal between us. When I thought I was going to die, I knew you would save me. We were of one mind.

For an instant, we were of one soul. We are meant to be together."

Rayna smiled. "I felt it, too."

Morgan's body was beaten up, and he ached all over, but Rayna's words made everything feel better. He could see in her eyes that she understood what he meant. They had learned they didn't need a vacation. They needed the experience of life—to the brink of death—together.

He kissed her and said with a slight tremble in his voice, "I love you."

"I love you, too," she whispered. "I'll always love you."

The End

"Lord Walmsley." It was Admiral Flan Kearn, my fleet commander, on the speaker. "We're approaching Pharry, and it's chaotic as hell in the atmosphere. Are you sure we should proceed?"

I drew in a determined breath. It was time. After Ostarand had conquered the majority of Eurania, Mapooly emerged from the far reaches of the star cluster with his Belaanian army. He defeated Ostarand in a head-to-head confrontation, drove the Revolutionary Guard across Eurania during a year-long campaign, and laid siege to Ostarand's home planet of Pharry. Two days ago, we intercepted signals that the month-long siege had finally broken through. The fighting had moved planetside.

I had to see the final outcome for myself, with my own eyes. This could be the end of the war. Would Mapooly emerge victorious and end the killing? Twenty-six long years—my entire adult career—and that following six centuries of outside occupation and disorder. Could we Euranians finally achieve a stable, lasting peace?

"Hold position, Admiral. I'm on my way."

* * *

Admiral Kearn and three of his assistants greeted me with sharp salutes. Together, we mounted the steps to the command platform overlooking the operations deck, where my eye caught the chaotic mess of ships filling the wraparound viewer that surrounded the bridge on three sides. Below our position, General Mapooly's dreadnoughts descended through the atmosphere while scores of landing craft emptied from both sides of the many troop carriers. As Mapooly's ships invaded, tiny vessels of all shapes and sizes—hundreds, perhaps thousands, of private craft—fled the planet in all directions. It was total pandemonium, a frenzied abandonment by those who could, while Mapooly's followers streamed in.

Captain Pavon met Admiral Kearn and myself on the command platform. "Sir, we have received a request for identification."

I smiled at Kearn. We could have said we were rejoining the People's Army, yet again. But why? "Let's see if we can slip in." I turned to Pavon. "Tell them our comm unit is damaged. Toss them a couple bursts of static."

Kearn gave Pavon a knowing nod. "Order the other ships to hold position out of detection range, Captain, and then take us down to the capital. Let's land somewhere outside the dome. Maybe the Agrian Fields, if it's not already taken."

"Yes, sir," Pavon said, departing to relay the order to the crew...